Phantom Unmasked

By Tracey West

SCHOLASTIC INC.
New York   Toronto   London   Auckland   Sydney
Mexico City   New Delhi   Hong Kong   Buenos Aires

ISBN 0-439-80000-5

Published by Scholastic Inc.
SCHOLASTIC and associated logos are trademarks and/or registered trademarks of Scholastic Inc.

12 11 10 9 8 7 6 5 4 3 2   6 7 8 9 10/0

Designed by Bethany Dixon
Printed in the U.S.A.
First printing, January 2006

Drew's Warning

May pushed her way through the glass doors of the Pokémon Center. "Yay! We're here!" she called out cheerfully. Her bright blue eyes sparkled with excitement.

May's friend Ash smiled. When he first met May, she wasn't interested in Pokémon at all. She was even a little afraid of them. But then she started entering Pokémon Contests with her cute Normal-type Pokémon, Skitty. May wanted to enter every contest she could. Ash and his friend Brock agreed to go with her. Her little brother, Max, came along with them, too.

And now they were in Verdanturf Town, the day before a Pokémon Contest. They could rest and get a meal at the Pokémon Center while they were waiting.

"Hey, look!" Max said, pointing across the room.

A green-haired boy was talking to Nurse Joy. She held a Roselia in her arms. The Grass-and-Poison-type Pokémon had fainted.

"I hope you can help me, Nurse Joy," the boy was saying.

"Drew! I knew you would be here!" May cried. May and Drew had been competing in contests together. Drew was still smarting after losing to May at the contest in Fallarbor Town.

"Oh, hello, May," Drew said. But he didn't bother to turn and look at her.

"I take it you'll be entering the big contest tomorrow?" Brock asked.

"I was, but I'm not anymore," Drew replied.

Drew's voice sounded sad. Ash looked at the Roselia in Nurse Joy's arms. It was Drew's favorite Pokémon, and it looked hurt.

"What's wrong with Roselia?" May asked.

"It got hurt battling," Drew said quietly.

"You mean you *lost*?" Ash blurted out. He didn't mean to be mean, but he couldn't help it. Drew thought he was the best Pokémon Coordinator around — and he let everyone know it. Ash thought Drew was even more obnoxious than his own rival, Gary.

"I don't think Roselia will be well enough to battle tomorrow," Drew said. He didn't take his eyes off of Nurse Joy. "I'll have to skip the contest tomorrow."

May gasped. Drew *never* missed a contest!

Drew finally turned around to face them.

"Here's a little advice for all of you," he said. "Watch out for a masked Coordinator who goes by the name . . . Phantom!"

Then Drew walked away without another word.

May's face turned pale. Ash knew exactly why she was worried.

If this Phantom had beaten Drew, how was May supposed to beat him?

Ash vs. the Phantom

Ash, Brock, and Max followed May as she hurried outside the Pokémon Center. Ash's yellow Pokémon, Pikachu, rode on Ash's shoulder. May stopped in a shady area on the green lawn. Then she held up a Poké Ball.

"I can't believe there is a Coordinator here that is stronger than Drew," May said nervously. "I've got to practice!"

"Please," Ash said. "If I knew where this Phantom guy was, I'd battle him myself."

May threw the Poké Ball into the air. "Go, Skitty! Come on out and take the stage!"

A Pokémon that looked like a cute kitten popped out of the ball. Skitty had a round face, pink ears, and a pink round puff on its tail.

"The Pokémon Contest is tomorrow, Skitty," May said. "We can win if we try!"

But Skitty was too busy chasing its tail in circles to listen to May.

"So why don't we practice your new Blizzard attack?" May suggested.

That got Skitty's attention. It stopped chasing its tail, opened its mouth, and a freezing blast of wind and snow blew out. The out-of-control attack blasted May and the others.

"May! Stop it!" Max yelled.

"Skitty, not like that!" May cried.

Skitty stopped the attack. May sighed with relief. "Good job. We don't need to work on Blizzard any-more," she said. "Let's work on your Doubleslap."

May took five small orange balls from her backpack.

"I'll toss the balls to you one at a time and you try to juggle them," May said.

"The way you use your attacks is the key to winning the first round of any Pokémon Contest, right?" Max asked.

"That's right!" May said. "So, Skitty, are you ready?"

Skitty wagged its tail. May threw out the first ball. Skitty bounced it on its tail. Then May threw out the next ball, and the next. Soon Skitty was juggling all five balls at once!

Then, suddenly, the balls tumbled to the ground.

"Oh, well," May said. "Let's give it another try."

But before May could try again, a light wind blew across the lawn, followed by a strange voice.

"You with the Skitty. Are you planning to enter the contest?"

The voice belonged to a boy standing with his back to May and the others. It seemed as though he had appeared out of nowhere.

"What do you care if I'm entering the contest?" May asked.

The boy turned around. He wore a black suit and a cape, like a magician, and a top hat. A strange mask covered his face. It was gray with one round, red eye in the center.

"The Phantom has but one purpose, wherever he goes," the boy said dramatically. "To battle!"

Ash stepped forward. "If it's a battle you want, I'll battle you!"

"You seem very sure of yourself," the Phantom replied. "I like that."

Ash and the Phantom stepped out onto the lawn and faced each other.

"I'll be the judge of this match," Brock offered. The older boy was training to be a Pokémon breeder. He had judged many of Ash's unofficial battles.

The Phantom nodded. "Standard contest rules. The battle will be five minutes."

"Okay!" Ash agreed. "I'm going to choose Pikachu to start."

Pikachu crouched at Ash's side, ready to battle.

"And as for me, I'm using Dusclops!" the Phantom cried.

The Phantom threw out his Poké Ball. A gray Pokémon about as tall as Ash popped out. Its face looked just like the Phantom's mask. It had a thick, gray body with stubby legs and large hands. Two long gray winglike arms came out of its back.

"What's that?" Ash asked. He had never seen a Dusclops before. He took out his Pokédex to get more information.

"Dusclops, the Beckon Pokémon," the Pokédex reported. "Dusclops is said to suck practically anything into its body, the black-hole-like core of which is completely empty."

Ash wasn't sure what to do. Dusclops sounded pretty strange. He decided to start off strong.

"Pikachu, take it down with Quick Attack!" Ash yelled.

Pikachu raced across the field. Its jagged tail blazed with bright energy.

Slam! Pikachu collided with Dusclops with tremendous force. But the Pokémon didn't fall.

"What happened?" Ash asked, amazed. Pikachu's Quick Attack almost never failed.

"Ash, that isn't going to work," Max piped up. "Dusclops is a Ghost Pokémon. Normal attacks aren't going to have any effect on it!"

Before Ash could change his strategy, the Phantom called for an attack.

"Go, Dusclops! Shadow Punch!" he yelled.

Dusclops's fists began to glow with misty gray light. The Ghost-type Pokémon charged at Pikachu, then . . . *BAM!* It punched the little yellow Pokémon with its left fist. *BAM!* It punched again with its right.

Pikachu reeled from the blows.

The Phantom held up his gloved hands. "Dusclops, finish it off with . . ."

The Phantom stopped and looked toward the street. A blue car came speeding toward them.

"Not now!" the Phantom cried. "Return, Dusclops!" He held out his Poké Ball, and Dusclops disappeared inside.

"Hey, what's going on?" Ash asked.

"We'll call it a draw," the Phantom said. Then a mysterious wind blew up.

When the wind died, the Phantom was nowhere in sight.

The Hunt for the Phantom

3

The car screeched to a halt. A plump woman with short brown hair jumped out.

"Oh, no, you don't!" she yelled. "You're not getting away from me this time!"

The woman ran into the wooded area, right behind where the Phantom had been standing.

"What's going on?" May asked.

"I don't know," Ash said. "But I want to find out!"

Ash and his friends ran after the woman. They saw her trip and fall. When she got back up, she was holding a pencil with a Poké Ball eraser on top.

"Aha!" she cried. "A clue!"

"Are you all right, ma'am?" Ash asked.

"I'm fine," she replied. "But you kids are *not* going to be fine if I find out that you are friends with that lousy masked Coordinator!"

"What are you talking about?" May asked.

"Don't play dumb," said the woman. "What have you done with my son, Timmy?"

The woman picked up Ash by the collar. "Tell me! Tell me!" she yelled. "Tell me what you and that masked Coordinator are up to — or else!"

Brock put a hand on her shoulder. "Lady, we had never even seen this Phantom guy until now," he explained.

"Yeah," May said. "He appeared out of nowhere and wanted to battle us."

The angry look vanished from the woman's face. She let go of Ash. "I'm so sorry," she said. "My name is Mrs. Grimm. I'm just so worried about my son,

Timmy. Lately he's started skipping school. I hired a detective to follow him. The detective noticed that everywhere Timmy went, this strange Phantom character turned up."

Mrs. Grimm sat down on a nearby park bench.

"I see why you're so upset," Brock said.

"Maybe you kids can help me," Mrs. Grimm said. "I want you to find out the identity of this Phantom guy. You're all Pokémon Trainers, so you can get close to him."

"You want us to take off his mask?" Ash asked.

Mrs. Grimm nodded. "I'll reward you, of course," she said. "Money is no object!"

Then she held up the pencil. "The Phantom dropped this," she said. "He scratched his hand on a sticker bush. I think the pencil is Timmy's. I'd like to take you all to talk to Timmy. Maybe he can tell us why the Phantom had his pencil."

From a nearby bush, a boy, a girl, and a Pokémon

watched the scene. The girl, Jessie, had long magenta hair. The boy, James, had periwinkle-hued hair. Meowth, the Pokémon, looked like a cream-colored cat with a jewel in the middle of its forehead. The three worked for Team Rocket, an evil organization devoted to stealing Pokémon.

Meowth was staring at the diamond rings on Mrs. Grimm's fingers. "Check out the bling-bling on Timmy's mom," he said dreamily.

"She'll pay us just for unmasking the Phantom?" James asked. "That'll be a piece of cake!"

"A twenty-four karat cake!" Jessie added.

Team Rocket watched as Ash and his friends followed Mrs. Grimm to her home. The three villains followed behind.

The hunt for the Phantom was on!

Timmy's Story

4

Mrs. Grimm led the friends up the steps to her home — a sprawling mansion.

"Welcome to my humble home," she said. She walked through the front door and began to call out. "Timmy! I'm home!"

A minute later, a pale, thin boy with sandy-brown hair walked down the marble staircase.

"Mom, when did you get home?" Timmy asked. "I was just upstairs studying."

Mrs. Grimm beamed with pride. "This is my Timmy," she said.

"Hi, I'm Ash from Pallet Town," Ash said.

"*Pikachu!*" Pikachu said.

The others introduced themselves, too.

"Nice to meet you," Timmy said. Then he turned and started back up the stairs. "Now, if you don't mind . . ."

"Hold on!" Mrs. Grimm said firmly. She held up the pencil with the Poké Ball eraser. "You wouldn't be missing something, would you?"

"Hey, where did you find my pencil?" Timmy asked.

"Aha!" Mrs. Grimm said. "I knew it was yours. Then explain why I found it when I was chasing the Phantom in the woods today."

Timmy suddenly looked nervous. "I don't know," he said. He reached out his hand to grab the pencil.

Mrs. Grimm gasped. "Timmy, you have a scratch on your hand! Where did you get that?"

"Nowhere," Timmy answered. "I'll be in my room, okay?" Then he quickly ran up the stairs.

Mrs. Grimm sat down on the couch. "This is all very strange," she said. "Timmy has a scratch on his hand, exactly where the Phantom got scratched today. Could it be that Timmy and the Phantom are the same person?"

"Just because they both have scratches doesn't prove anything, Mrs. Grimm," Brock said.

Ash couldn't imagine that pale, quiet Timmy and the forceful, confident Phantom were the same person. "The Phantom is an awesome Coordinator," Ash said. "Has your son been studying to become a Pokémon Trainer?"

"Of course not!" Mrs. Grimm snapped. "Timmy is going to take over my company someday. I won't let him waste his time on that Pokémon nonsense."

"You can learn some important lessons by interacting with Pokémon, Mrs. Grimm," Brock pointed out.

"I don't need your advice," Mrs. Grimm said. "Your

job is to find out who the Phantom is — that's all!" Then she stomped out of the room.

Max grimaced and sat down on the couch. "I'm sure glad she isn't *my* mom," he said.

"I almost feel sorry for Timmy," May added. "He didn't look happy."

"You're right," someone said. "He's really not a happy boy."

A man walked into the room. He looked like an older version of Timmy, with a sad face. He sat down in a chair.

"Who are you?" Ash asked.

"I'm Timmy's father," the man replied. "Tommy Grimm is my name."

"So then you're Mrs. Grimm's husband?" May asked.

Ash frowned. He couldn't imagine what it would be like to be married to someone as rude as Mrs. Grimm.

"I heard what my wife asked you to do," Mr. Grimm said. "I can probably help you solve that little mystery. Follow me."

Curious, the friends followed Mr. Grimm to a room at the far end of the mansion. Mr. Grimm opened a closet door to reveal a Phantom costume — a black suit, cape, top hat, and Dusclops mask. The costume was faded and fraying.

"Are you telling us that *you're* the Phantom?" Ash asked, amazed.

"That costume's too old," Brock said.

"I can explain," Mr. Grimm began. "When I was younger, I was quite a good Pokémon Coordinator. Then I fell in love with Mrs. Grimm. We were perfect for each other, except that she hated Pokémon. She made me promise never to allow them in the house.

"But I loved Pokémon so much, I couldn't keep my promise. I made this Dusclops costume. Whenever I could get away from Mrs. Grimm, I would enter Pokémon Contests as the Phantom!

"Eventually, I gave up being the Phantom. Then Timmy was born. He loved Pokémon, too. One day he found a lost Duskull, and he brought it home. But his mother wouldn't let him keep it."

"How sad!" May said.

Mr. Grimm nodded. "I knew I had to help Timmy. So I made him a new costume. And I let him raise the Duskull in secret. Duskull evolved into Dusclops. And Timmy became the new masked Coordinator — the Phantom!"

"Wow," Ash said. "So that's what's going on."

"When Timmy becomes the Phantom, he's not shy anymore," Mr. Grimm said. "Being a Pokémon Trainer is good for him. I just wish my wife would agree with me. And now she's close to finding out the truth. . . ."

Ash could not imagine how his life would be if

his mother had forbidden him to become a Pokémon Trainer. He never would have met Pikachu, or gone on his journey, or met any of his friends.

"Maybe we can do something to help," Ash said.

Brock smiled. "Listen up, everybody," he said. "I think I have the perfect plan."

A Phantom Plan

The friends followed Mr. Grimm to Timmy's room.

"Son, you have some company here," Mr. Grimm said, opening the door.

"Dad, no!" Timmy cried. He quickly tried to hide his Phantom costume.

"It's all right," Mr. Grimm said. "You don't have to hide anything from these guys. They're your friends."

"How would you like to enter tomorrow's

Pokémon Contest?" Ash asked. "Without your mom suspecting anything?"

"Are you serious?" Timmy said. "I'll do *anything* to enter that contest!"

"Then here's what we have to do. . . ." Brock began.

A little while later, the friends put their plan into action. May and Max stood in front of the door of the mansion. May let Skitty out of its Poké Ball. As soon as she saw Mrs. Grimm's car pull up to the door, she threw the orange balls at Skitty.

"Come on, Skitty. Use Doubleslap to juggle," she coaxed.

Mrs. Grimm got out of her car and frowned. "What is that Pokémon doing here?"

But a voice interrupted her. "Hey, down there! How would you like to battle me!"

The Phantom appeared on a balcony above the front door. But it wasn't really the Phantom — it was Brock, dressed in the Phantom costume!

"It's him again! It's the Phantom!" Mrs. Grimm shrieked.

Ash and Pikachu ran onto the scene. "May, what's wrong?" Ash asked.

"The Phantom is back again!" May cried.

Then the front door burst open. Timmy and Mr. Grimm stepped out.

"What's all this about the Phantom?" Timmy asked.

Mrs. Grimm looked at the Phantom, then she looked at Timmy. "But I thought *you* were the Phantom, Timmy!"

"Mom, are you feeling all right?" Timmy asked.

Ash smiled. Their plan was working perfectly! If Mrs. Grimm was sure that Timmy wasn't the Phantom, then Timmy could enter the contest without worrying about getting caught.

"Well, if no one is going to battle me, I'm leaving," Brock said from the balcony. Then, suddenly, he felt a tug on his Phantom mask. "Hey, what's going on?"

Ash looked up. Brock's mask was attached to a fishing line, which was attached to a fishing pole, which was attached to Team Rocket! They stood on the third-floor balcony.

"Prepare for trouble — the Phantom's exposed!" Jessie said.

"Make it double as our bank account grows!" James added.

Jessie threw out a Poké Ball. "Now we will unmask the Phantom and collect the reward! Seviper, go!"

A Pokémon that looked like a long black snake with red fangs burst out of the ball. James threw a Poké Ball next.

"Cacnea, you attack, too!" he yelled.

A round green Grass-type Pokémon with sharp spikes flew out of the ball. It hugged James with its spiky arms.

"No, not me!" James cried. "That hurts! Attack the Phantom instead!"

"Seviper, use Wrap on the Phantom," Jessie ordered.

Seviper wrapped its long body around Brock. He couldn't move his arms at all.

"Get this thing off me!" Brock yelled.

James tugged on the fishing line.

"Now get that mask off and reveal the Phantom," Meowth urged.

"It's not coming off," James complained.

Timmy turned to Ash. "Do something!" he begged.

"I can't use one of Pikachu's Electric attacks," Ash said. "The attack might hit Brock — I mean the Phantom — too!"

"Cacnea, get that mask off," James yelled.

The green Pokémon jumped down toward Brock.

"Oh, no, you don't!" May cried. "Skitty, use Blizzard!"

Skitty blasted the balcony with a ferocious, freezing wind. Jessie, James, Meowth, Seviper, and Cacnea flew off the balcony and landed in their balloon, which hovered nearby. Brock flew off the balcony, too. He landed in a heap on the Grimms' lawn. May ran to his side.

"Are you all right?" she asked.

Ash grinned. *Now* he could take care of Team Rocket.

"Pikachu, finish them off with Thunderbolt!"

"Pika! Pika!" Pikachu said eagerly. It hurled a huge blast of electricity at Team Rocket's balloon.

Wham! The attack sent Team Rocket spiraling off into the distance.

"Looks like Team Rocket's blasting off again!" they cried.

Then Ash noticed Mrs. Grimm. She was walking toward Brock. His Phantom mask had been knocked askew during the fall.

"Oh, no . . ." Ash whispered.

But Brock quickly replaced the mask. Then he jumped to his feet.

"The Phantom strikes again!" he said, laughing an evil laugh. Then he ran off into the bushes.

Mrs. Grimm looked stunned.

"So I guess we'll never know the Phantom's true identity," May said.

"But we know for sure it can't be Timmy," Ash added.

Everyone watched Mrs. Grimm. Had she believed their act? Had she seen Brock's face?

"Of course it's not Timmy," Mrs. Grimm said. "Now, if you'll excuse me, I have to get back to work."

Mrs. Grimm walked into the mansion. Brock came out of the bushes.

"How'd we do?" he asked.

"Somehow it all worked perfectly," Ash said.

"All right! That means you're in the clear, Timmy," Brock said.

Timmy grinned. "That's so great! Thanks, guys."

May faced Timmy. "This means we'll see each other in the contest tomorrow."

"We sure will," Timmy said. "And I plan on winning!"

"Oh, yeah? Well, we don't plan on losing," May said. "Right, Skitty?"

"Skitty!" the cute Pokémon replied.

Ash hoped May was right. He had battled Timmy and knew he was tough to beat.

Could his friend really beat the Phantom?

The Amazing Jesslana

6

The next day, May signed up for the Pokémon Contest in the lobby of the contest arena. Ash, Brock, and Max stood by her. The lobby was crowded with Coordinators and their Pokémon. Ash knew that every one of them was hoping to win.

"Why am I so nervous? It's not like this is my first time competing," May said.

Skitty mewed and rubbed its head against May's legs.

"But it is my first contest with you, Skitty," May said. "Oh, I hope I'm ready for this!"

Ash scanned the crowd. "Timmy's late," he said. "He's going to miss the deadline for entering the contest. I can't believe he would let that happen."

"Pika! Pika!" Pikachu pointed toward the door.

Timmy ran in, out of breath. "Sorry I'm late," he panted.

"Hurry up and register!" Ash urged.

Timmy signed up at the desk just in time. Then he returned to his new friends.

"My mom gave me a bunch of extra homework to do just before I left," Timmy explained. "I think she still suspects something."

"So how did you manage to get away?" May asked.

"My dad helped me sneak out," Timmy said. "I just hope I can find a way to make it up to him someday."

"I can tell you how to do that, Timmy," Ash said. "Do your best today. That'll make him proud."

"I'll try," Timmy said. Then he put on his Phantom

mask and laughed mysteriously. "Come on, May! Let's show them what a really great Coordinator can do!"

Timmy and May left to go backstage, where they would wait until it was their turn to compete. Ash, Brock, Max, and Pikachu took seats inside the arena. They were just in time. The audience lights dimmed, and a spotlight shone onstage. A woman with curly blond hair walked out.

"Welcome, ladies and gentlemen, to the Verdanturf Town Pokémon Contest!" she cried. The crowd clapped and cheered. "I'm your host, Vivian Meridian!"

Vivian introduced the judges: Mr. Contesta, Suziko, Director of the Pokémon Fan Club, and Nurse Joy. Then she reviewed the format of the contest.

"In the first round, all competing Coordinators will be judged on how well their Pokémon complete their moves. Style counts in the first round," Vivian began.

"In the second round, the four best Coordinators

will face each other in a five-minute battle. The judges will subtract points from each Coordinator as the battle goes on," the host continued. "Finally, the last two Coordinators will battle one-on-one. May the best Coordinator win!"

The crowd cheered again.

"Now let's meet Coordinator number one . . . Jesslana!" Vivian announced.

A girl in a yellow coat and black boots walked out. She wore a tall gray hat on her head. Ash and his friends didn't know it, but Jesslana was really Jessie from Team Rocket! She always entered contests in disguise because she knew the police were always on the lookout for her.

"I'll be starting out with Dustox!" Jesslana cried. As she said the Pokémon's name, she tossed a Poké Ball into the air.

Dustox, a Toxic Moth Pokémon, flew out of the ball. It had a purple body and bright green wings. It

landed gently on top of Jesslana's hat, and she imme-
diately struck a pose.

"Isn't that beautiful, folks?" Vivian asked. "Striking,
majestic . . . a perfect opening statement!"

The crowed clapped, impressed.

"I'm just getting started!" Jesslana said. "Dustox,
Poison Sting!"

Dustox spit white poison darts from its mouth.
They filled the air onstage.

"Follow up with Whirlwind!" Jesslana said
quickly.

Dustox flapped its wings, and the poison darts
whirled and swirled until they became graceful
circles.

"And now Psybeam!" Jessie shouted.

Glowing rays of light poured from Dustox's body.
They hit each of the twirling circles, making them
glow and twinkle like stars. The crowd gasped in
amazement.

"Unbelievable! Dustox used Whirlwind to lift Poison Sting high into the sky, and then set it aglow with Psybeam!" Vivian cried. "An impressive combination of techniques, folks!"

In the audience, James and Meowth cheered Jessie.

"Way to go, Jessie!" James yelled.

"Hey, it's Jesslana," Meowth reminded him. "You're going to blow her cover!"

Back onstage, the judges typed in their scores. Each judge could award up to ten points for the round.

"Jesslana's score is twenty-eight point five," Vivian announced. "An almost perfect score! That will be a tough act to follow!"

Ash felt nervous about May's chances. The Phantom was good. But Jesslana was really amazing.

"She'll be tough to beat," Ash said, worried.

7

A Busted Blizzard

Backstage, May grew more and more nervous. She watched as the other contestants took the stage. Finally, she heard Vivian call out her name.

"Next up, contestant twenty-one. Let's hear it for May!"

May walked out onto the stage. The bright lights blinded her for a moment. Her palms sweat as she gripped her Poké Ball.

"Let's go, Skitty!" she cried, tossing up the Poké Ball. "You're up!"

Skitty popped out of the Poké Ball and landed gently on its four paws on the stage floor.

"All right now. Blizzard, Skitty!" May yelled.

Skitty opened its mouth to start the Blizzard attack.

Nothing came out but a puff of cold air!

The crowd groaned.

"What a shame," Vivian said. "May's very first technique has completely failed."

May frowned. "My nervousness must be affecting Skitty," she commented. "Now we've got to make up for that. So, Skitty, use your Doubleslap!"

May tossed the orange balls to Skitty one at a time. Skitty juggled the balls expertly, not dropping a single one. The crowd went wild.

"Now let's see what the judges have to say," Vivian said. "Here's the score: twenty-four point nine."

"That's not high enough to beat that Jesslana," Ash remarked to Brock.

"May still might have a chance," Brock said. "She just has to get one of the top four scores in this round."

Then the Phantom took the stage. He waved his cape, and Dusclops appeared.

"Dusclops, Will-O-Wisp!" the Phantom cried.

Dusclops opened its palms. Glowing balls of blue light appeared in the air in front of the Ghost-type Pokémon. Each glowing ball had a flaming tail.

"Follow up with Psychic!" the Phantom commanded.

The glowing balls began to rise in the air. They formed a spiral shape, and then began to move in circles. The effect was dazzling. The crowd erupted in applause.

"Wow! A mind-bending combination of Will-O-Wisp and Psychic from the Phantom!" Vivian cheered.

Then Vivian announced the judges' score: "Twenty-seven point eight — Let's hear it for the Phantom, who finishes the first round beautifully!"

The Phantom took a bow.

The rest of the Coordinators took their turns. Then everyone waited to find out which four Coordinators would move on to the next round. Ash, Max, Pikachu, and Brock went backstage to see May.

"Messing up Skitty's Blizzard attack really cost me big-time," May said sadly.

"Aw, don't worry," Max said. "Your score was still good."

Suddenly, Vivian's face appeared on a big screen in the locker room.

"Attention, please!" Vivian said. "We now have the final word from the judges. Contestants moving to the second round are Jesslana, Stefano, the Phantom, and, finally . . ."

May closed her eyes. Did she make it?

". . . May, for a total of four!"

May opened her eyes and let out a happy scream.

"*Pikachu!*" Pikachu cheered.

"Great job, guys," Ash said.

"Now it gets really tough," Brock added.

"I know," Timmy said. He turned to May. "But we're friends no matter what, May, right?"

"Sure," May said. "May the best Coordinator win!"

No More Secrets

8

"Welcome back to the second round: Contest Battles," Vivian announced. "Victory is awarded to the contestant who, in five minutes, can take away more of his opponent's points."

May stood on the stage, facing Stefano, a dark-haired boy wearing a gray turtleneck. His Wartortle, a tough Water-type Pokémon, stood next to him.

"First up, May versus Stefano! Begin!" Vivian cried.

"Skitty, use Doubleslap!" May shouted.

Skitty pounced into action. It bounded across the

stage and then began slapping Wartortle with its pink tail.

Bam! Bam! Bam! Bam! Wartortle had no way to respond with a counterattack. It fell to the floor and fainted.

"Wartortle is unable to battle," Vivian said. "May and Skitty will proceed to the final stage!"

May pumped her fist in the air. "All right! Skitty, you were awesome!"

"Way to go, May!" Ash yelled from his seat in the audience. Then something made him stop.

Mr. and Mrs. Grimm walked up the aisle and stood by the stage.

"It's Tim's mom!" Ash said. "I hope she doesn't suspect anything."

The Phantom and Jesslana took the stage next.

"Let the battle begin!" Vivian cried.

"You better watch out," the Phantom taunted. "Dusclops and I are unbeatable."

"Please," Jesslana said. "We're going to beat you without batting an eye — pardon the pun!"

Jesslana made the first move. "Go, Dustox! Whirlwind now!"

Dustox flapped its wings, and a powerful wind whipped through the stage. Dusclops stood still, unable to move.

"Whirlwind has immobilized Dusclops!" Vivian said.

"Shadow Punch, Dusclops!" the Phantom shouted.

Dusclops pushed through the Whirlwind and punched Dustox hard.

"No way!" Jesslana cried.

A screen above the stage showed a picture of Jesslana and the Phantom. Under each one's picture was a yellow bar that showed how many points they had. After the attack, Jesslana's bar became shorter.

"Jesslana's points have taken a serious hit," Vivian said.

But Jesslana wasn't ready to give up. "Dustox, Psybeam now!"

Dustox flew above Dusclops. The Ghost-type Pokémon wasn't expecting an attack. Bright blue beams shot out of Dustox's eyes and slammed into Dusclops. This time, the yellow bar under the Phantom's picture became shorter.

"Now Jesslana fights back and takes points from the Phantom!" Vivian cried.

"The battle's not over yet!" the Phantom said confidently. "The Phantom doesn't know the meaning of defeat!"

"Dustox, use Psybeam again," Jesslana said.

"Dusclops, use Psychic!" the Phantom commanded.

Blue beams shot from Dustox's eyes again. A white beam shot out from Dusclops's single, red eye. The powerful beams met in midair, each one pushing against each other.

"Keep pushing it back!" Jesslana yelled to Dustox.

"Dusclops, don't give up!" the Phantom called out.

Both Pokémon pushed harder. Then, without warning, the two colliding beams exploded in the air! Thick black smoke filled the stage.

When the smoke cleared, Dustox had fallen to the stage. And Jesslana's disguise had fallen off, revealing Jessie's red hair and Team Rocket uniform!

"Hey! It's Team Rocket!" Ash yelled.

"Time is up," Vivian said. "The winner on points is the Phantom and Dusclops! They will compete in the final round."

Jessie scowled. "That's what I get for playing fair and square," she said. "Now I'll just have to take your Dusclops by force!"

"I don't think so!" the Phantom said.

Then James and Meowth jumped up onstage.

"Prepare for trouble, Mister Mystery," Jessie said.

"Make it double, because you're history!" James finished.

Ash jumped to his feet. "Go, Pikachu! Thunderbolt them!"

Zap! Pikachu quickly blasted Team Rocket with a powerful Thunderbolt attack. The force of the attack sent Jessie, James, and Meowth flying backward.

"Aaargh!" Jessie moaned. "That will be the last time I ever try to win anything without cheating!"

"Back to our usual plan?" James asked.

"Yeah," Meowth said. "Cheatin' without winnin'!"

Then the three villains cried out together. "Team Rocket's blasting off again!"

Pikachu's powerful Thunderbolt had another effect. It had sent Timmy's mask flying off of his face. The crowd gasped.

"The Phantom's mask is off! His face is revealed!" Vivian cried.

Mrs. Grimm's eyes filled with tears. "Timmy! It's you!"

Then she ran out of the arena.

9

May vs. Timmy

Timmy ran backstage, upset. Mr. Grimm followed him. Ash and the others gathered around.

"Now she'll never let me battle again!" Timmy wailed. "Why does Mom hate Pokémon so much?"

"Believe it or not, your mom loved Pokémon when she was young," Mr. Grimm explained. "She even had a Poochyena that she took care of. But her parents wanted her to grow up fast so she could take over the family business. They made her give up her Poochyena, and she was forbidden to have contact with Pokémon ever again."

"I never knew that," Timmy said. "That's so sad."

Mr. Grimm nodded. "Your mother just thought that if you never fell in love with Pokémon, you'd never have your heart broken . . ."

". . . like she did," Timmy finished.

Mr. Grimm nodded. "It looks like she can't bear to see you with your Pokémon, Timmy," he said sadly. "This could be your last chance to be in a Pokémon Contest. So you'd better make the most of it! Go get 'em!"

Timmy nodded. "All right, Dad. You can count on me!"

Ash went back to his seat. He hoped his friend May would win. But whatever happened, it was going to be a great battle!

Timmy put his mask back on. Then May and the Phantom took their places onstage.

"Begin the battle!" Vivian cried.

"Dusclops, Focus Punch!" the Phantom yelled.

Dusclops made a fist, and a white ball of glowing

light came out of its hand. The light ball flew across the stage and slammed into Skitty.

"Mew!" Skitty cried.

"Skitty, time for your Doubleslap!" May yelled.

Skitty jumped on Dusclops and began slapping the Ghost-type Pokémon's eye with its tail. But Dusclops wasn't affected at all.

"Remember, May!" Max called out from his seat. "Normal attacks won't work against Dusclops!"

The Phantom continued the assault. "Dusclops, use Focus Punch again!"

Dusclops made another fist. Another white, glowing ball hurtled toward Skitty. . . .

"I'm in trouble," May muttered. Then she had an idea. "Skitty! Send it right back with Doubleslap!"

"Mew!" Skitty said happily. It turned around and expertly batted the Focus Punch back to Dusclops.

The crowd cheered.

"What an impressive counterattack!" Vivian said. "May hits the Phantom with his own Focus Punch!"

"Way to go, May!" Brock yelled.

The Phantom tried a different attack. "Dusclops, Will-O-Wisp!"

Dusclops opened its hands, and four teardrop-shaped masses of blue light appeared.

"Now follow with Psychic!"

The Psychic attack helped push the blue balls of light toward Skitty. They lunged at the tiny Pokémon, striking Skitty again and again.

In this battle, pictures of May and the Phantom were displayed on the screen. After this attack, the yellow bar under May's picture became shorter, showing her lost points. May clutched both of her fists in frustration.

"If Normal attacks are worthless, how am I supposed to battle him?" May wondered. But she had to do *something*. "Skitty, Tackle attack!"

Skitty charged across the stage at Dusclops.

"Dusclops, use Hyper Beam now!" the Phantom shouted.

A yellow, pulsating beam shot from Dusclops's red eye. The beam slammed into Skitty before it could tackle Dusclops.

Max shook his head in disbelief. "May's still using Normal attacks," he said.

"And she's losing," Ash added.

Losing points just made May angry. "I'm not going down without a fight!" she cried. "Skitty, Blizzard attack!"

Skitty opened its mouth. But instead of a punishing wind, only a small puff of air came out — just as it had in the first round.

"Not again!" Ash wailed.

"Dusclops, Hyper Beam, go!" the Phantom ordered.

The Phantom sent another powerful Hyper Beam racing at Skitty. The beam hit the little Pokémon with full force.

"May has lost more than half her points," Vivian said. "Will she be able to turn this around?"

"I've got nothing left to do," May muttered. She searched her mind. All she had were Normal attacks. Except . . .

"I still have one attack!" May said.

Dusclops launched another Hyper Beam at Skitty.

May reacted quickly. "Skitty, use Assist!"

The crowd gasped. Ash couldn't believe it. Assist was a risky attack. When a Trainer called for Assist, the Pokémon could respond with any attack at random. May had no idea what Skitty might do. It might help her — or lose the battle for her in one instant.

Skitty jumped up and opened its mouth wide. A huge blast of air poured out. The forceful wind knocked back the Hyper Beam.

"That's not fair!" the Phantom protested.

10

May's Bold Move

"Good for May," Brock remarked. "You never know what the results will be with Assist. But at least now May has a chance."

"Way to hang in there, May!" Max called out.

The Phantom frowned. "That Assist attack sure took me by surprise," he muttered. "I've got to finish her off quick! Dusclops, Focus Punch now!"

"Assist!" May shouted.

Dusclops aimed a Focus Punch at Skitty. Skitty jumped up, and long strings of energy came from its mouth. The strings wrapped around the glowing Focus Punch and disabled it.

"Assist became String Shot this time!" Vivian cried.

The Phantom frowned. "I have to stop her. But how? I don't have a clue!"

"Timmy!"

The Phantom turned. His mother, Mrs. Grimm, stood onstage behind him. Was she going to stop the battle?

"Don't ever collapse under pressure, Timmy!" she called out.

"Mom?" Timmy asked, surprised.

"Dusclops is battling for you because it trusts you," Mrs. Grimm told her son. "Just like May's Skitty trusts her. Have confidence in yourself, and faith in your Pokémon, and then you won't need a mask!"

"Yeah! You're right," Timmy said. He took off his mask and threw it on the floor. Then he smiled at his mom.

Ash and his friends watched the scene from the audience.

"Now Timmy knows that his mom is on his side," Max commented.

"That's good," Ash said.

Brock nodded. "And it will make the battle an even better one!"

Timmy turned back to May. "All right, then. Let's go!"

"You bet! Let's both give it our all!" May called back.

"Dusclops, Will-O-Wisp!" Timmy shouted.

Dusclops sent four balls of blue flame toward Skitty.

"Assist, Skitty, do it!" May said urgently.

Skitty shot back with a barrage of hot, glowing embers. They quickly broke up the Will-O-Wisp.

"Ember this time, cool!" Ash said.

May called for Assist again. This time, Skitty launched a shining attack called Silver Wind.

"Dusclops, Psychic!" Timmy called out.

The Ghost Pokémon launched a series of Psychic beams. They quickly shot through the Silver Wind, breaking it up.

"This battle is tied, and there are only seconds on the clock!" Vivian said, her voice filled with excitement.

"There's no way I'm losing after what it took to get this far," Timmy said to himself. "One last attack should finish her off."

May gritted her teeth. "It's just too much to expect Assist to come through for me again," she said. "I'm going to have to put all my faith in Skitty!"

Timmy called for his best attack. "Go, Dusclops! Hyper Beam!"

"Now, Skitty! Blizzard!" May called out.

Ash was shocked. Blizzard? Skitty hadn't been able to use that attack once during the contest!

Skitty jumped up in the air. It opened its mouth wide. . . .

A truly massive blast of freezing wind and snow exploded out, knocking Dusclops on its back!

"Dusclops, no!" Timmy cried. But it was too late.

"Time is up!" Vivian announced. "The victory goes to May and her Skitty!"

May picked up Skitty. "We won! And it's all because of you, Skitty!"

"*Mew!*" Skitty said happily.

May and Timmy stepped into the center of the stage and shook hands.

"Congratulations, May," Timmy said. "But there's no way I'll ever lose to you again."

"Oh, yeah?" May replied, smiling. "We'll just have to see about that."

Mrs. Grimm walked up and hugged Timmy. "Both of you were really great."

Timmy looked at the floor. "I'm sorry about sneaking out," he said.

"That's all right, son," Mrs. Grimm said. "I understand."

"You do?" Timmy asked.

Mrs. Grimm nodded. "And as long as you don't fall behind in your homework, you can continue to enter these Pokémon Contests."

Timmy hugged his mom again. "Thank you so much! I love you so much!"

Ash, Pikachu, Brock, and Max joined May onstage. The judges walked to the center of the stage and faced May.

"And now the judges will present May and her Skitty with the prized Verdanturf Ribbon," Vivian announced.

One of the judges placed an orange ribbon in May's hand. May grinned.

"I can hardly believe it, but we did it, Skitty," May said.

Ash smiled at his friend. He knew how she felt.

"Winning is great," Ash said. "And having great Pokémon you can count on is even better. Right, Pikachu?"

"*Pikachu!*" Pikachu agreed.